Books by the same author

Cup Final Kid

Fred the Angel

Little Obie and the Flood

Little Obie and the Kidnap

Our Sleepysaurus

For older readers

The Dump Gang

My Aunty Sal and the Mega-sized Moose

MARTIN WADDELL

Illustrations by David Parkins

WALKER BOOKS
AND SUBSIDIARIES
LONDON • BOSTON • SYDNEY

For the children of Scoil Mhichil Naofa,
Athy, County Kildare

First published 1997 by
Walker Books Ltd, 87 Vauxhall Walk
London SE11 5HJ

This edition published 1998

2 4 6 8 10 9 7 5 3 1

This book has been typeset in Garamond.

Printed in England

British Library Cataloguing in Publication Data
A catalogue record for this book
is available from the British Library.

ISBN 0-7445-5406-3

Contents

Who's in It

This is Lord Reginald Parrot, aged eight, eating very big buns.
Buns come in big sizes when you are rich, like Lord Reggie.

This is Lord Reggie's tiny friend Skinny Atkins, aged six. He is poor. There are things you don't do if you are poor and one of them is: *you don't ask a Lordship for one of his buns*. That's why Skinny hasn't a bun … but look at those muscles!

This is Lord Reggie's old aunt, the wicked Aunt Parrot who is scheming to get Reggie's money, ripping the sails of *The Crimson Parrot* with her ship-wrecking knife, so the ship would blow on to the rocks.

Lord Reggie Parrot at Bay

One day Aunt Parrot rode up to Parrot Cove in her carriage.

"Woe is you, Reginald baby," she told Lord Reggie. "Some bad person ripped the sails of *The Crimson Parrot* so the ship would blow on to the rocks. Your dad and mum have been lost at sea. With any luck they've been eaten by sharks. Ha-ha-ha!"

"Oh woe indeed!" Lord Reggie cried and he almost choked on his bun. Then he took a fresh one and cheered up.

"That means I get all their money when I grow up!" he said, and he began figuring out what he would buy, for starters, with all the Parrot dough – a chain of hamburger joints and a bun shop and three trillion jam tarts and…

"*If* you grow up!" Aunt Parrot hissed under her breath. She had plans for Lord Reginald Parrot.

"Can I have some of my own money to spend now, please?" Lord Reggie asked politely.

"No dice, Reginald baby!" cooed Aunt Parrot. "For now, I look after all your money for you, which translates as: I spend it on me! That means it won't go to waste on good causes and orphans!"

“But that isn’t fair!” gasped Lord Reggie. He didn’t care much about the good causes, but he was an orphan

himself now … or he *thought* he was, because that’s what Aunt Parrot had told him.

“Who says life has to be fair?” cackled his wicked old aunt and she sent him to play with the new butler she’d brought with her, named Nark, and Lord Reggie’s new nanny, Nanny Dogwash.

This is Nark …

and this is Nanny Dogwash.

(Don't ask where Nanny Dogwash caught her hat. You don't want to know that.)

"Now I am rich, I want to go out and eat," Lord Reggie told Nark and Nanny Dogwash.

"You ain't going nowhere, little Lord Reggie!" hissed Nark. "Me and old Nanny Dogwash is here to see you stay in and die of natural causes, so your aunt won't have no bother when she goes to sign up for your money."

They locked fat Lord Reggie up in the dungeon under the West Wing.

Nark fixed a ball and chain round Lord Reggie's leg and secured the chain to the wall. It wasn't meant to be comfortable, and it wasn't. If he picked up the ball Lord Reggie could hop a bit, but not very far – and there was always the risk that he might drop the ball on his toe.

And he *did*!

It was Lord Reggie's hour of pain and despair *but*... Someone brave heard the scream and set out to rescue His Lordship.

MY POOR TOOOOOOOOOE!

The sun set on Parrot Cove, the moon rose, and Lord Reggie was sitting alone in his dungeon dreaming of apple tarts and cream truffles and counting the spiders who spun on the wall.

Then...

Lord Reggie looked up, and he blinked.

"Who's there?" squeaked Lord Reggie, springing to his feet to see where the tapping came from.

The tapping sound seemed to come from the floor, under his feet.

Suddenly one of the great stone slabs in the floor lifted and out popped…

If you can't guess who it is, you'll find out on the next page→

The Rescue of Lord Reggie Parrot

"Good fellow, Atkins!" cried Lord Reggie, grabbing the bag of cream buns Skinny Atkins had brought him.

"I've come to rescue you, Your Lordship," Skinny panted, touching his forelock. "With Your Lordship's permission, of course."

"Permission granted, Atkins," said Lord Reggie, sitting down on his ball. It was very heavy to hold when he stood up, so he hadn't been standing up often. It wasn't very comfortable to sit on either, but he managed it, while he was wolfing his buns.

Skinny set to work, hacking the iron ring out of the wall. It was a great relief to Lord Reggie when he was freed. The chain was still fixed to his leg, but at least he could walk round the room with his chain in his hands and Skinny to carry the ball. That is what servants are for.

"Oh-er-ooh... I fear Your Lordship is too fat to squeeze down my tunnel," Skinny said nervously.

But there are things you don't do if you are poor, and one of them is: *you don't tell a Lordship he's fat*. But Skinny was brave and the situation was desperate, so he did it.

Lord Reggie looked cross.

"I meant to say *my tunnel's built too small for a Lordship*," Skinny said quickly. "I wasn't suggesting your Lordship is chubby. Everyone knows you are slim for a Lordship."

"Then how do you propose I escape, Atkins?" Lord Reggie asked.

"When Nanny Dogwash brings your gruel, we jump her and fight our way out, if it pleases Your Lordship," Skinny suggested.

"Lordships don't fight, Atkins!" Lord Reggie said with disdain. "We leave fighting to common persons, like you."

"As Your Lordship pleases," sighed tiny Skinny.

So, when Nanny Dogwash came with the gruel…

(Isn't the way that hat eats disgusting? Don't ask what sort of creature it is – you don't want to know that.)

"Quickly, Your Lordship!" Skinny cried.

"Lordships don't run from danger, Atkins," Lord Reggie replied coolly.

"Permit me to do the running, Your Lordship," Skinny said.

Skinny carried Lord Reggie piggyback up the stairs, which was just fine for Lord Reggie.

"Halt in the name of wicked Aunt Parrot!" cried the guards, barring the way with their swords and...

"All done, Your Lordship," Skinny panted. "You can open your eyes."

Lord Reggie opened his eyes.

The brave two were on top of the battlements above Parrot Cove, but just then the burglar alarms started ringing and all the lights flashed on and someone screamed...

"Jump, Your Lordship!" Skinny cried, but His Lordship looked down at the moat far below.

"No, Atkins!" said Lord Reggie coldly. "Lordships don't jump. You, of all people, ought to know that."

Lord Reggie Parrot in Peril

There are things you don't do if you are poor, and one of them is: *you don't push Lordships off the top of their battlements*, because Lordships don't like it. But Skinny was brave and the situation was desperate, so he did it.

His Lordship and Skinny wound up in the moat far below.

"You pushed me, Atkins!" Lord Reggie spluttered, when Skinny hauled him to the surface.

"Your pardon, Your Lordship," said Skinny. "It wasn't exactly a *push*. My foot slipped."

"Swim Atkins!" ordered Lord Reggie.

Skinny didn't want to be told that Lordships don't swim; they are swum *with*. He swam as hard as he could for the bank, pulling Lord Reggie and his ball and chain along behind him.

That was fine, but it made him slow in the water. Slower, for instance, than Aunt Parrot's crocodiles.

Aunt Parrot, on the battlements, had just pulled a lever that released them for a feast of Lord Reggie, washed down with a tiny bit of Atkins. (There only could be a *tiny* bit of Atkins, because that was all there was.)

Crocodile teeth grazed Lord Reggie's chin.

That's when Lord Reggie really showed his Lordly cool. He kept his nerve, as only a Lordship can do.

"Attend to the crocodiles, Atkins!" Lord Reggie ordered.

"But Your Lordship, I need both hands to keep you afloat!" Skinny gurgled. (Gurgling happens when you've swallowed a lot of water, which Skinny just had.)

"Use your feet, Atkins!" Lord Reggie said, closing his eyes tightly. "Don't panic, boy! Your Lordship's in charge!"

"All clear now, eh Atkins?" Lord Reggie sighed, as Skinny pulled him up on to the bank, along with his chain and his ball.

"Mind the arrows, Your Lordship!" yelled Skinny, as a rain of deadly arrows hummed through the air.

"Aunt Parrot's at it again!" Lord Reggie said, with a shake of his head.

"Duck, Your Lordship!" cried Skinny.

"Lordships don't duck," Lord Reggie replied. "*Do* something, Atkins! At once, if you please."

Lord Reggie Parrot Pursued

There are things you don't do if you are poor, and one of them is: *you don't hide a Lordship under a dead crocodile*. Lordships need to be seen to be brave, and they can't be seen under a croc. It just isn't done. But Skinny was brave and the situation was desperate, so he did it.

"Atkins!" Lord Reggie cried. "Lordships don't save their skins from arrows this way!"

"Dead crocodile suits you, Your Lordship," gasped Skinny. "The scales match the gleam of your glory!"

"Well I suppose that's true," admitted Lord Reggie.

The arrows flew down all around them as the pair staggered on, under the croc. Skinny was carrying Lord Reggie, complete with his chain and his ball, and Lord Reggie was covered in croc, so they didn't get hit.

They ran …

and they ran …

and they ran,

pursued by a wolf pack unleashed by Lord Reggie's wicked old Aunt Parrot. The wolves howled and snarled, hot on the trail of Lord Reggie's skin.

“Run faster, Atkins!” ordered Lord Reggie coolly.

“I’m running as fast as I can, considering I’m carrying you, you great berk!” Skinny muttered. (He thought it was under his breath.)

There are things you don’t do if you are poor, and one of them is: *you don’t call a Lordship a berk.*

But Skinny was brave and the situation was desperate and anyway, Skinny was so fed up with Lord Reggie that he just went and said it, risking his all.

They never sorted it out because by this time Skinny was head down and panting, with a crocodile leg over his eyes, so he didn't see the edge of the cliff as the wolves chased him towards it…

"Stop, Atkins!" Lord Reggie wailed. "Lordships don't run off cliff-tops!" But Lord Reggie had spotted the peril too late.

Skinny Atkins ran right off the top of the cliff…

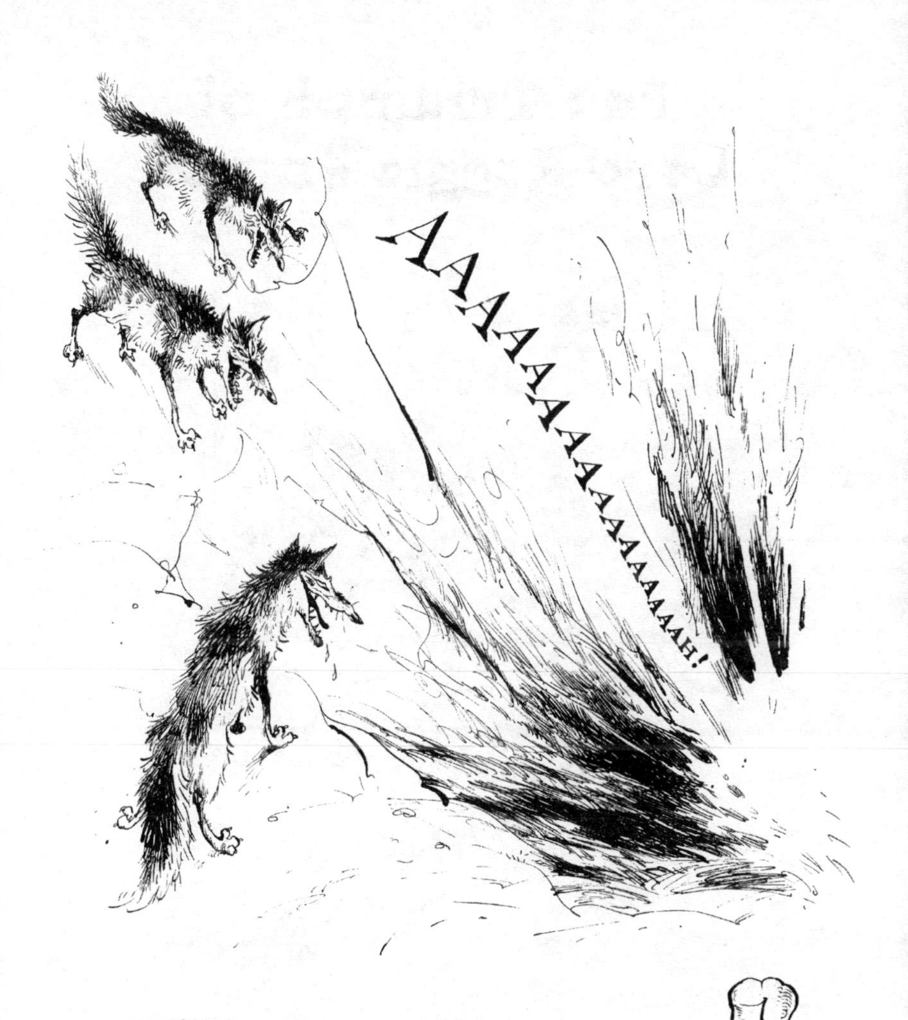

If you want to know how
Lord Reggie was saved, that bit
is on the next page ⟶

The Triumph of Lord Reggie Parrot

They were falling …

and falling …

and falling …

and falling…

"Saved!" Skinny cried, as they lay on the deck of a ship, washed up on the rocks, with the waves crashing round it.

"Lordships *are* saved," Lord Reggie calmly replied. "It goes with the business of being a Lordship."

"I know this ship!" Skinny gasped. "This ship is *The Crimson Parrot*, Your Lordship."

"See to those scruffy persons tied round the mast, Atkins," Lord Reggie remarked.

"But Your Lordship, those scruffy persons aren't persons," said Skinny. "Those persons are Lordships like you." (Skinny knew a Lordship when he saw one. He could tell by the bossy look on their faces, under the seaweed.)

"My goodness!" Lord Reggie cried. "It is my *pater* and *mater*, not drowned at all."

(Lordships don't say *dad* and *mum*. Lordships say *pater* and *mater* instead. It is Latin. All Lordships know Latin. If you didn't know that, now you do.)

In a trice Skinny had freed them, and Aunt Parrot's evil plan was undone. She had left Reggie's *pater* and *mater* to drown in the wreck of *The Crimson Parrot*, so she could nip off and nab Reggie and snaffle their money.

"Man the guns, Atkins!" Lord Reggie cried, as a dark ship appeared out of the storm, hard to port. It was Aunt Parrot's ship, manned by her foul crew, led by Aunt Parrot and Nanny Dogwash and Nark.

But Aunt Parrot's ship sailed on through the cannonballs Skinny was firing.

"Fight to the last man, Atkins!" Lord Reggie roared and he turned and ran, as the villains leapt on board.

Skinny didn't bother to ask who the last man was.

He just knew.

Then...

CRASH!
WALLOP!
BANG!
SMASH!
CRASH!
WALLOP!
BANG!
PING!
PONG!
BOOM!
BONG!
YAROOOOH!

"All done, Your Lordship!" Skinny gasped, throwing Aunt Parrot into the sea. She was a meal for the sharks with the rest of her crew, along with Nanny Dogwash and Nark. "All done."

"All done, Atkins? I fear I think not!" said Lord Reggie.

Of course Skinny knew what he meant. Lordships need tea *at once* when their work is all done. That is what Skinny knew.

There are things you don't do if you are poor and one of them is: *you don't tell Lordships to make their own tea*. So Skinny made a tea of cream buns and rum for Lord Reggie and his *pater* and *mater*.

Skinny rowed everyone home before he had his tea, but it turned out all right because Skinny's mum made him buns when he got home. They weren't Lordship-type buns, they were better.

That is the end of the story.
But if you want more, see below

Yes, *Pater* and *Mater* were Pirates, not Parrots! So their ship should have been called *The Crimson Pirate.*

Skinny Atkins knew that, but one thing you don't do if you're poor is: *you don't tell Lordships how to spell their names…*

And→

This time Skinny kept his mouth shut.